# DICKENS'

## *Friends* Reflections of
a Therapy Dog Team

*By*
**Judie Freeland**

i

# Dickens' Friends

ISBN-10: 0990482669
ISBN-13: 978-0-9904826-6-6

Library of Congress Control Number:
2015955225

Penstemon
Publications
Wellington, Colorado

# *Dedication*

In memory of Dickens' friends who are gone and dedicated to those who are still here.

This book could not have happened without the encouragement, support, and thoughtful criticism of the Penstemon Publications writing group: Bev, Clare, Gary, Libby, Mim, Nancy B., and Nancy P. Thank you all.

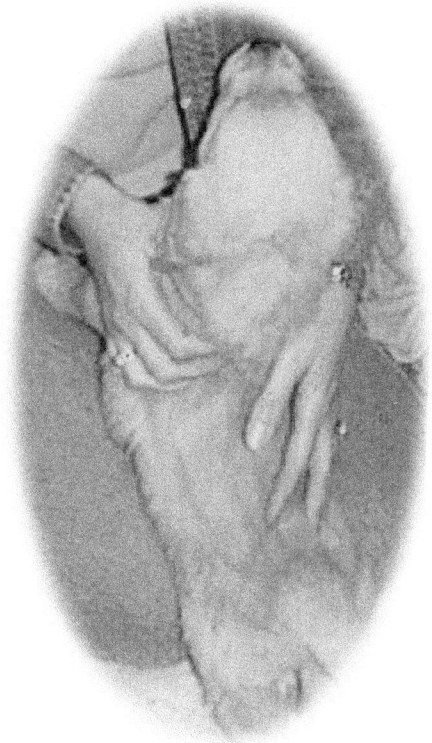

*"Little Dickens"*

# *Foreward*

Real people inspired the characters in this book. However, to respect the privacy of individuals and their friends and families, the names, descriptions, and story details have been altered.

# Contents

# *Contents* continued

# *Laura*

*You're antsy. I promise I'll be really good. I'll do everything just like I did on the tests.*

< I know you will. But this lady is 102 years old, so she's really fragile. You can't put a paw on her knee or accidentally scratch her with your nails.>

Dickens rolled his eyes. *You know I wouldn't do that. Let's go meet her.*

I was a bit concerned that Dickens might jump on the bed and inadvertently hurt Laura, but I remembered the advice of a friend: "Trust your dog as he trusts you."

I tapped on the door and in we went.

*Is this her whole house? It's very nice, but really small. Our bedroom is bigger than this.*

Dickens was right. However, the room was nicely decorated with a handmade quilt on the bed with pillow shams and an easy chair patterned in the same soft blues, greens, and pinks. The dresser and matching dressing table were well-cared for antiques. The only item that seemed out of place was the walker near the head of the bed. Floor space was at a minimum.

As Dickens would soon see, however, most rooms of this size had two occupants, a curtain dividing the living space near the window from the other half, near the door.

Laura was sitting on the edge of her bed. Snow-white hair and the wrinkles to prove her age, but that smile! It twinkled in her eyes as well. She barely glanced at me; her full attention was on my Dickens, my golden retriever, my newly certified therapy dog.

"Come here, you lovely thing," she said.

We moved closer. Dickens put his head in her lap and focused his eyes on her face. For several minutes, Laura murmured sweet nothings as she stroked his head, the cowlick between his eyes, the top of his neck, his shoulders. "Oh, you are such a good boy. You like that? A little farther back? Such a good boy."

*I am such a good boy. And she's such a good lady. What's 'such' mean?*

We could have stayed all afternoon, but we had many more people to visit. "Dickens, we need to say good-bye for now." Reluctantly, he turned his head away from Laura. She looked up, her hand still on his head. "Thank you for coming."

"We'll be back," I promised. "We come every week."

At that the luminous smile was back. "I'm glad. I'll look forward to seeing you both again."

Dickens slowly moved away and, without being told, came to a nice heel. As we neared the door, his head swiveled back to Laura and his tail wagged gently.

*I love that lady. And she loves me. Was I good?*

< Yes, love, you were wonderful.>

*She's wonderful.*

At our next visit, a few minutes after I sat down on Laura's bed near her feet and Dickens put his head in her lap, Laura looked up, although her hands continued caressing Dickens' head and ears. "I wonder what he's thinking about."

*Not thinking at all. Simply enjoying the love that moves from hands to my head to my heart. And I think she can feel me returning the favor. I'd give her a real hug, except I might hurt her, so this is the best I can do.*

<I think it's just what her doctor ordered.>

"Laura," I said, "Judging by the look on his face, I'd say he's thinking how very much he loves you. You're one of his very special people."

She beamed and leaned over to kiss the top of Dickens' head. He couldn't resist. Seeing her head so close, he very softly licked her closest ear.

As always, Laura's room was our first stop. When we entered, Laura was sitting on the side of her bed, talking to an elderly man. As soon as she saw Dickens, out came the smile. "David, here's the dear dog I told you about. This is my son David," she said, looking at me. "He came to have lunch with me."

I made all the right noises and realized with a jolt that the elderly man had to be about my age. I tended to forget that Laura was over one hundred.

David said his goodbyes and Laura's attention quickly shifted to Dickens. "Such a good dog. You like your ears scratched, don't you? "As usual, his head rested on her lap, his eyes on hers, both of them oblivious to anyone or anything else.

*Such gentle hands, and she knows just where to scratch and how hard. Could she come to our house for a visit? Other friends do.*

<I'm afraid not, Dickens. She's here because she's frail and needs trained medical help close by.>

A few minutes later Cindy, one of the CNAs, came in to help Laura use her walker to get to the bathroom. We prepared to leave. When Laura sweetly thanked Cindy for helping her and Cindy said, "It's a pleasure," I realized she really meant it. Laura was the kind of person people wanted to help.

Although we usually spent at least ten minutes with Laura, this day our stay was brief. She smiled apologetically as she said she was having trouble breathing. I checked to make sure her oxygen lines were clear and as we left, I told Lisa, one of the aides, that Laura was in distress.

*She'll get better, won't she?*

<I don't know, Dickens. We'll pray.>

A week later, we weren't able to visit. In response to my tap on her door, one of the aides opened it, saying, "I'm sorry. Laura can't see you today. Her daughters are here, and two hospice people. Laura's in a coma."

The next time, Patsy met me at the front door. "Laura died the day after you were here last week." I thanked her for letting me know, composed myself and started

4

down the hall. Dickens stopped at her door, eyes sparkling and tail wagging.

<She's not there, dear. She's gone.>

He whimpered, but obediently came to heel and we moved on.

The following week, Dickens stopped at Laura's door again. I opened it so he could see that it was empty. He looked all around the bedless, chairless, pictureless room. His ears and tail drooped.

*Gone.*

Once more, Dickens stopped briefly at the door that no longer bore Laura's name plate, shook himself as if remembering, and moved ahead. Others still needed him.

Laura's room, which now was someone else's, was in the assisted living wing of Evergreen Manor. Although Dickens and I go to Evergreen three times a week, we can't see all our friends on the same day. The residents in assisted living see us Monday afternoons. Wednesday is our day for the adult day care center in another part of town, followed by a stop at Evergreen's physical therapy center. On Fridays, we see friends in hospice care before entering the nearby locked, curtained glass door leading to the dementia ward.

I tried to explain the differences to Dickens.

*I get it. Some friends try to give me cookies, some know I prefer ice cubes. But they all like to pet me.*

<It's a bit more complicated than that.>

*You mean like some have hurt arms or tummies and some have heart hurts.*

&lt;That's a good way to put it. And they tell us their stories.&gt;

*We hear their souls.*

# Arthur

During the months after Dickens' first visit as a newly certified therapy dog, we made many new friends and got reacquainted with a few old ones.

Arthur, a tall, handsome man in his mid-fifties with a warm smile that reminded me of Gregory Peck, used to enjoy the visits of Dickens and other therapy dogs to the assisted living wing. Arthur welcomed brief chats with the human handlers, although dementia prevented him from remembering conversations. He spent his days walking the halls, sitting in the lounge holding hands with Janice, and occasionally taking short walks outside with her.

Janice's blue eyes, curly blond hair. voluptuous figure, and a sweet smile made her the perfect counterpart for Arthur's good looks.

He never remembered her name, or anyone else's except his own, but she was his girlfriend and Dickens was "a good dog."

Arthur took one outside walk too many, without Janice. He's now in the dementia wing, where the way out is a door that opens only to the correct key code.

The first time I entered that area, I was apprehensive.

## Dickens' Friends

Would Dickens frighten these people? Would one of them try to hurt him? I needn't have worried. As soon as the door shut behind us, Dickens' tail started wagging. *New friends! This man likes me!* What had been the blank stare of a person whose mind was not functioning was now lively eyes in a smiling face.

Each person we encountered momentarily came alive. I wondered what they remembered – a beloved pet, perhaps? Dickens looked at me. *They remember love.*

Arthur still walks the halls and still smiles when the good dog comes in for a visit.

# *Janice*

Janice also walks the halls, but not because she doesn't know where she is. She knows she needs to keep exercising. She's not trying to get out of here. She likes it. "The nicest place I've ever lived. I'm trailer trash. Raised in a rusty old mobile home that would never be mobile again. Everything in it was filthy, full of junk. Junk littering the floors and in boxes that weren't going anywhere. Refuse on the floors, the table, a TV that didn't work; dishes that were never going to be washed if I didn't do them."

Janice's half of her tiny room was spotless and tastefully, if sparsely, decorated.

*It smells nice in here. Not so nice near the door. Whoever else lives here has peed on the carpet. But it's nice here near the windows. This lady friend smells nice, too. I love her.* As usual, Dickens had his head in Janice's lap, tail moving like a metronome.

Janice hadn't mentioned her past life on previous visits, but today she wanted to talk. "Even when I was little, I tried to keep my own room clean. When I was about ten, someone gave me a padlock for my door. No one else had a key. My clothes were clean; I stopped at the laudromat every Thursday on my way to school and loaded my t-shirts, underwear, and jeans into a washer.

**9**

It had to be Thursday, because Mrs. Armbruster did her laundry on Thursdays, and she'd put my stuff in a dryer and loosely fold it into my basket when it was done, ready for me to pick up after school.

"It was Mrs. Armbruster who called the police and the ambulance that morning when I passed out at the door."

Dickens looked up at her, concern in his chocolate brown eyes. *She hurts. Her chest hurts. Her legs and feet hurt really bad. Old hurts, still there. Inside hurts, too.*

"What happened?" I asked.

"The woman I once thought was my mother hit me. The others decided it looked like fun, so they joined in. One of them had a bat. I don't know – and I don't care – what happened with those other people. All I know is that when I got out of the hospital, I couldn't go back. The doctors said my body would never be right again. A nice policeman said there was no place to go back to. He brought me here and here I've stayed. Nicest place I've ever lived."

# Stella

Halfway down the next hall, we found Stella, smiling as the tears ran down her face. "I don't know what was worse, hearing that your Echo was gone, getting kicked out of that other place while I was in the hospital, having to give my cat away, or then being sent to drug rehab. Here is better, but if it hadn't been for your friend John, I wouldn't have lasted more than a week. Too many people. I hate this place. In that other home, at least I had a room to myself.

"But enough bitching. So this is Dickens. He's grown so big since you came to see me right after you got him."

*I climbed in bed with her and we snuggled.*

"I didn't know if you'd remember," I said. "You were just back from surgery and you were pretty woozy."

"I don't remember much of that whole week, but who could forget a warm puppy snuggling close? I kept hoping you'd come back. And then they sent me away."

*Tell her!*

"We snuck in that time," I said. "We've visited John whenever we could; if you'd still been here, we would have come to see you too, but for visits to our other friends here, we had to wait until Dickens was old enough to take the Therapy Dog tests and go through the evaluation process. As of last Friday, we're now an official team. We'll be able to come every week."

*We could come every day. Couldn't we?*

"I'll count the days," Stella said. "My daughters usually get here on Saturdays. You know they live in Windsor but work in Denver? Well, anyway, that'll be two days a week to look forward to, and John's got me playing Bingo with a bunch of folks on Sundays in the dining room.

*Bingo? That nutty springer spaniel?*

<No, dear. Bingo is a card game. Hard to explain.>

Stella looked at Dickens. "Don't tell me that dog plays Bingo?"

I laughed. "No, but he knows the name. There's a hyperactive dog in our neighborhood that goes berserk as it runs along our back fence, dragging its person on the other end of a leash."

Diane, one of the CNAs (Certified Nurse Assistant), poked her head in the door. She wanted to meet Dickens. I try to warn people that getting down on his level is asking for trouble, but I wasn't fast enough. A mutual hug session ensued, until Diane finally stood up.

*New friend! Young, like a puppy. Strong. Not sick.*

"Can he have a treat?" she asked.

"Only if you have access to an ice cube."

"Stay here. I'll be right back." Soon she returned with a paper cup full of Dickens' favorite treats. "One at a time or all at once?"

*One. And another one. And another one. Not all*

*dumped on the floor. I take them carefully from fingers.*

"One at a time," I replied, "and ask him to sit for each one."

Stella watched in delight as Dickens fastidiously took each of a dozen ice cubes from Diane's fingers. I winked at her. "You do realize, Diane, that he will now expect his very own cup of cubes every time he sees you," I said.

*Wasn't that what she planned? She likes me. Now she knows I like ice cubes. Expecting her to remember the next time is a no brainer.*

"Giving him ice cubes gives me a moment of joy. We don't get a lot of those moments.. Nor do the residents."

The last time we saw Stella, she was out of her bed for the first time in months and sitting in a chair. Dickens put his head in her lap and looked at me, tail whipping from side to side. *She's happy! Something nice has happened.*

"Guess what?" she said, eyes sparkling. "My daughters have found a house that's handicap accessible for us to share, and I'm moving there next week."

Dickens had become resigned to friends disappearing from their rooms and rarely returning. He'd stop and check their former beds and sigh. *Gone.* But the next time we visited Stella's old room, he sniffed the empty bed, smiled that incredible golden smile, and wagged his tail. *Stella's room. It still smells happy.*

# John

John and I had been friends for several years. We met when I visited Evergreen Manor with my previous therapy dog, Echo, gone now to the Rainbow Bridge. I hoped that Dickens would, after some maturing and training, follow in her paw prints. He'd been very good so far with new people; it was time for him to relax a bit with another old friend, one he'd met a week after I brought him home.

<Shall we go see John?>

*Yes, please. Best friend John!*

A year earlier, at nine weeks old and twelve pounds, Dickens was the just the right size for laps. He would not be old enough to be an official therapy dog until his first birthday, but I persuaded the activity director that John needed a puppy hug. He deeply loved Echo and still mourned her passing. Dickens cuddled on the man's lap as big hands stroked his little body.

We visited John a few more times as Dickens got bigger – and began to show that he understood the need to be calm and gentle with vulnerable people. He wasn't rough with John, but neither was he the sedate, laid-back, serious creature that he is with more fragile friends.

# Dickens' Friends

Now Dickens and I were an official therapy dog team and Dickens knew which people were most vulnerable and with whom he could be a bit more rambunctious. We were barely in the main door when he spotted John in the living room area and soon had his front paws on either side of the footrest of John's wheelchair and his head halfway up John's chest for a hug.

*Good hugs. Good friend. If he could get out of that chair, we could roll on the floor and wrestle.*

"We'll have to do our wrestling while I sit here, little friend," John said. (Apparently, I'm not the only one who "hears" Dickens.)

*Who you calling little?*

John is a big guy. At that time, a really big guy, about 350 pounds of big guy. With very gentle big hands for the dog he loves. Serious health issues sidelined this one-time long-distance semi driver, who admits to being a hellion in his younger days.

Today is a good day and a very boyish grin lights up his 80-year-old face as he talks about a long ago fishing trip with buddies – lots of fish, lots of beer, lots of stories, and a long-suffering dog who preferred, John says, to be retrieving ducks.

*I'm a retriever. I could retrieve ducks.*

Residents aren't allowed to smoke in their rooms for obvious reasons, but the aides understand they can't take away what small pleasures are left to people whose health is already compromised; one risky habit isn't going to make much difference.

John was out by a picnic table with Tom, Bobby, Dottie, and Stella, all of them happily puffing away. Dickens' tail wagged furiously, but he stopped a couple feet away from John's chair and simply looked – first at the cigarette in John's hand, then at his face, then back to the hand. "What's wrong, Dickens?" John asked.

*I thought it was obvious. Don't like smoke. Makes me choke. Makes you cough.*

John extinguished the cigarette and wiped his hands on his jeans. "Sorry, chum. Come closer and let's talk about it. The rest of you people need to put out your smokes if you want Dickens to say hello."

There was some mock grumbling - "Damn dog wants to deprive us of the only pleasure we have," Tom muttered, ditching his cigarette and clapping his hands. "C'mon here and say hi, Dickens."

When we stopped a couple weeks later, John wasn't in his room and it was too raw outside for the patio, so we kept going until we found him in the dining room. "Hi, John. I brought you a book." Since John liked adventure and mystery tales, I thought he'd enjoy Jeffrey Deaver, one of my favorite authors.

He reached for the book, but Dickens shoved his nose into the outstretched hand.

*First things first.*

John laughed and ruffled Dickens' head and ears. "Sorry, buddy, you're right. The book can wait. What's new in your world?"

Dickens laid his head in John's lap and for several

minutes, eyes locked, the two held a silent conversation. Whether it was about rabbits or the scent left by our neighborhood coyote or the new dog in the next block, I don't know. It was a private chat.

When they ended the exchange, John looked up at me, with the kind of look on his face that small boys wear when they've done something really clever. "I've lost another ten pounds, That's sixty so far since Labor Day. Another forty to goal!"

I clapped him on the shoulder. "That's great. You're looking good and your color is better. You finally convinced the kitchen staff that you seriously wanted salad and not French fries with dinner?"

"Well, I did have two French fries this noon. But no dessert."

"What was it?"

"Jello with fruit cocktail in it. I don't much care for it. And this is Friday, so there'll be ice cream as the afternoon snack." He grinned. "I get mine in a paper cup, so I don't have a cone to worry about."

I knew that even losing a hundred of his 350 pounds would not cure the diabetes that periodically sent him to the hospital to have the blood clots in his legs drained before they killed him. But it couldn't hurt and might even give him more time and less excruciating back pain.

"C'mon back to the room with me. You can take a look at my books and see if there's something you'd like to borrow."

He carefully set the Deaver novel on his bedside tray

alongside Tom Clancy's *The Sum of All Fears* that lay bookmarked halfway through. "I've got several Grishams down there," he said, pointing to the bottom shelf of a bookcase behind the door. You've probably read most of them, but maybe not any of the Stuart Woods. Help yourself."

I picked out a book and then, hearing the ice cream cart coming down the hall, said, "We'll leave you to your afternoon snack and go find the ice cubes. Thanks for the book. We'll see you next week."

As John and I were chatting one day a few weeks later, I asked if he knew Dottie. Dickens put his head on John's knee. *I know her. She smells a whole lot better these days.*

John ruffled the dog's ears. "Dickens, you're a bit of nag, you know. Just like my ex-wife. Smoking might eventually kill me; for sure, something will, but it's one of the few pleasures I have left."

Dickens sighed and cuddled in a bit closer. *I'm another one. I've heard you say that my visits are a real pleasure.*

"To answer your question," John said, looking at me, "Sure, I know Dottie. She used to join the rest of us smokers out in the patio, but then she quit. I don't see her so much anymore."

"Did she ever tell you that she drove a semi for some company in Indiana?"

"No kidding? I'll have to look her up and we can exchange tales of the road. I'm surprised – hard to picture that little bitty thing handling a mega-ton behemoth. I knew she was a feisty one, but that beats all. Real grit."

"What's your scariest or most interesting experience as a driver?" I asked.

"Well, let's see." He thought for a moment. "I guess it'd have to be the time I was north of the Wisconsin border heading for Chicago when my CB radio started connecting me with a bunch of guys who'd just heard a tornado warning. A big one was headed right toward us.

"One call got everyone's attention. An unfamiliar voice on the CB said, 'This is Swordfish. I'm on I-90 heading south, hauling a horse trailer. I got a mare and her new filly in there and they're starting to act freaky. Bad weather coming. Have you guys got any suggestions for me to ride this out safely?'

"I could see the little brown pickup about a mile ahead of me, weaving all over the road and gradually slowing down. The other guys all had suggestions, but we pretty quickly agreed that the fellow's only hope was us. We knew that you're supposed to avoid underpasses if there's a tornado around, but this stretch of road was really flat, and I had visions of that truck, trailer, mom and baby horse, and that poor guy being sucked up into the clouds."

*We would hide in the basement, wouldn't we? I like most of outside, but big winds scare me. If John saved those horses, he's a hero, isn't he?*

John continued, "I had actually met a couple of the other truckers, but I knew most of them only by their

CB handles. I got Danny of the Dunes and Salmon King ready to move ahead of the horse guy with Thundermaker and me pulling up the rear of our caravan.

"I told Swordfish to wait until two semis pulled ahead of him and then follow them under a big underpass coming up in just a couple miles. The sky was turning that ugly dark green that anyone with sense wants to be miles away from and it was dead still. By now, I was going about twenty miles an hour, and I was right on the tail of the horse hauler. I was relieved to see that it wasn't jumping all over the road anymore. I prayed that that mom and her baby would just stay real still until we were all safe.

"I saw Danny and King's rigs pull ahead of the pickup and close enough so bumpers were damn near touching. We crawled into that underpass and stopped, Danny's nose just peeking out the front and Thundermaker's rear end barely under shelter. That's the scariest trip I ever had."

*So then what happened?*

"Yes, John, then what happened?"

"Well I'm here aren't I? We sat there while a hundred freight trains roared over our heads and the winds tried to suck us out from under our cave. Then it got real quiet and be damned if the sun didn't come out. Just for a minute, but we could see the rainbow. And then it started to rain. Buckets of the stuff. But we were all okay. Swordfish was so nervous he stuttered as he thanked us. I followed him all the way to Ann Arbor and continued on my way to Detroit. I chatted a couple other times with the other truckers, but Swordfish and I never crossed paths again."

John and Dickens and I traded horse and hunting stories for the next several weeks. Then one day, John wasn't in his room or out on the patio. "He took a bad turn," Bobby told me. "He's in the hospital. Blood clots. Dickens can go there to see him, can't he?"

"Yes. We pass right by there on our way home."

Lying in a hospital bed almost too narrow for his big frame, John was nearly as white as the sheets. His normal ruddy color had fled. He was obviously weak, but very pleased to see Dickens.

*I can't get up in the bed with him, can I? Could this be one of those 'ceptions you always talk about?*

<No, dear. You might accidentally bump John's sore legs and make him even sicker.>

*I could lick his owies and make them better. Or are they all wrapped up like they sometimes are when we see him in his rolling chair?*

John looked up at me as Dickens laid his head on the bed near John's face. A face that had a smile on it and eyes that had a hint of twinkle. "I don't think there's room in this bed for both Dickens and me, but I'm definitely getting a mental snuggle. When I came here, I was ready to die, but Dickens assures me it isn't yet my time. You'll be at the place in a couple days? I'll be there soon."

And he was. By Thanksgiving, he'd lost another

twenty pounds and said he would keep going. "But not til after the holidays!"

There were two more crises during the next year that sent him to the hospital, and two or three times, Dickens and I found him in his bed, sound asleep. He never spent time in his room if he could help it.

*Is John sick again?*

<I hope not. Probably he'll be okay again next time.>

Sure enough, he was back holding court in the dining room, getting ready for Bingo. "I'm a tough old bird," he said when I expressed concern. "I'll be here for my birthday."

*A bird? John's not a bird. I know about birds. They're little and they're noisy and they fly. Remember that big black one that dive-bombed me? Protecting its babies, you said. Like I'd ever hurt a baby anything. Did he say birthday? I know about birthdays. Parties!*

"John, your birthday's the end of November, right?" I asked.

"That's right. Eighty-two years and most of them pretty good. Not too much to regret."

Two days after the birthday party, complete with peanut butter and ice cubes for Dickens, John was moved to the hospice wing, where after all the years, he had a room to himself – and his many visitors.

Often, however, he was asleep.

*I could wake him up.*

<Let's let him sleep. He doesn't hurt when he's asleep.>

# Dickens' Friends

*Is he going to sleep forever, like friend Laura?*
<Soon, yes.>
*And then he won't ever hurt again?*
<That's right. Never again.>

# *Rachel*

Rachel was moved to hospice the same week. Like John, she was a long-time friend. When we first met, she was in her late sixties, looking more like fifty, and absolutely gorgeous. Her long silver hair fell in loose ringlets under her hat. Not really a hat: a large brim of woven straw with only a band to keep it on the head, the kind of protective head gear some golfers wear that leaves the crown uncovered. Because it was flamingo pink, on anyone else it would have looked absurd. On Rachel it was elegant. She wore it constantly, partly to shade her eyes, partly to keep her hair out of her face.

*Why does she wear a hat inside?*

<Because it's pretty.>

*Yours isn't. Is that why you wear it only outside?*

<Yes. It keeps the sun off my face. It used to be pretty, a long time ago, but now it droops.>

For the first several years of our friendship, Rachel spent little time in her room, preferring to cruise the halls in her wheelchair and visit with people, or sit in the sun on the patio, or work on her weaving in the activity room. On Mondays, we usually found her waiting for us in the front lobby.

Our conversations ranged over several topics. One

day she asked, "I guess you're retired or you wouldn't have free days to visit this place. What did you do before?"

*You're retired? What's that mean? Tired again?*

<No. It means I don't work anymore.>

*But you do work. I can hardly get you to sit still long enough to pet me.*

<Yes, but I don't get paid for doing what I want to do and when I want to do it.>

*Oh. So if you don't get paid, is my dog food free?*

<We'll talk about it some other time. Rachel asked me a question.>

I told her, "I taught college English."

"Really? What kind?"

"Medieval literature."

The biggest smile I'd ever seen lit up Rachel's face. "Wonderful! You know 'La Chanson de Roland'?"

I would never have guessed that I would spend part of an afternoon visiting a nursing home in a lively discussion of twelfth century French poetry.

Dickens loves being the center of attention, but he recognizes those times when people need to talk about something else. When Rachel asked her question, he sighed and lay down. *You two go ahead and talk. I'll have a nap.*

During another visit, after greeting Dickens and accepting a soft lick on one ear, Rachel asked, "Have I told you about my dog, my Lad?"

*She has a dog. I knew I wasn't the first one she ever*

*met, 'cuz she knows just where to scratch behind my ears.*

"We'd love to hear about him, I said." Dickens turned around twice and lay down, ears perked up and ready for a story.

Rachel took a sip of water, lay back, and closed her eyes for a moment. "My husband was away – he was usually away – and the kids and I were alone on the little ranch we had, in our house on the hill. We had only one neighbor, a pleasant man who kept to himself mostly, but did tell me he would be gone for a few days and his brother might stop by to check that everything at his place was all right.

"I was out hanging the wash. Lad, the German shepherd my husband got me for protection, snoozed near the laundry basket. The six little dogs – Jack Russell terriers - played tag around the shrubbery. I heard a car needing a new muffler coming along the road and looked up in time to see it pull into my neighbor's driveway. I assumed it was the brother. But three rough-looking men got out and looked around."

Dickens got to his feet, neck ruff bristling. Rachel noticed and told him, "No one here, dear. It's just a story."

*Sorry. Didn't mean to interrupt. Then what happened?*

"One of them spotted me and made a comment to the others that had them all laughing. Not nice laughter. The three of them started coming up the hill toward me. The terriers stopped their game and started racing down the hill, yapping as little dogs will.

"The leader stopped to grab a loose tree branch and

waved it with menace toward the small pack. They turned tail and scooted back up the hill.

"I turned to look for Lad. Not by the clothes basket. He was on his way down the hill, toward the threat. Unlike the little dogs, he was not running. Nor was he barking. You've seen that German shepherd crouch, belly almost on the ground, back legs almost hidden, front legs moving one at a time as the dog slinks soundlessly toward prey?"

*I do that when I see a rabbit in our yard.*

"I couldn't hear Lad at first, but the volume of the low growl in his throat grew as he got halfway between me at the top of the hill and the men at the bottom. It took a minute for them to see Lad, less than that for them to hear him. They stopped. He continued stalking them. They apparently decided that whatever they'd had in mind was not such a good idea. Backing slowly to their car, the three got in and closed the doors. Lad rose to his full height, posing like the sentinel he was, watching as the car turned around and drove away. They did not return."

Rachel lay back, smiling, before she reached for the carafe of water.

"That's a wonderful story," I said. "How old was Lad?"

She thought for a moment. "He was just a pup when we got him, around Christmas one year. And this happened in summer, over a year later. So he'd have been a year and a half? He was twelve when he had the stroke."

She reached for a tissue, blew her nose, and took another sip of water.

Over the next several months, we talked about our children and grandchildren, places we'd lived or visited, people and pets we had known, and books we had read. We did not talk about her failing health.

One week, Rachel didn't meet us at the front door. She was in bed, propped up on several pillows, with a length of tubing leading from an oxygen tank to the cannula looped around her head and into her nose.

Dickens knew about tubing that snaked across floors and he was careful to step over it. *Friend Rachel hurts to breathe. But she'll get better, won't she?*

Rachel saw my look of consternation and assured me, "This is just temporary. My lungs are weak, but not too bad. I must have overdone it."

A few weeks later, we stopped to chat with Su, Rachel's roommate, who was sitting on a bench in the sunshine as we walked to the main door.

"Hi, Su. You picked a perfect day to be outside."

*She likes being in a warm sun bath. Me, too.*

<You like being outside in warm, cold, sun, cloud, rain or snow.>

Su put a marker in her book and leaned over to greet Dickens. "Yes, perfect. A good book, a quiet place, good friends to visit but not intrude."

I raised an eyebrow. "A bit too much inside today?"

She nodded. "Rachel's in one of her misery moods and won't stop moaning about her life. There's no es-

28

cape in the dining room – a well-meaning pianist who can't carry a tune howling out old war songs: 'When the Lights Go On Again,' 'Tipperary,' and others of that ilk."

*When we dogs howl, we have our reasons.*

"Patsy's just trying to provide activities to get people out of their rooms and socializing," I said.

"I know. And we do have the option of not participating."

"We'll leave you to your book and go see Rachel. When she's having a bad day, Dickens always cheers her up."

*Can I show Su my new trick?*

<Sure. Show her how you say goodbye and then you can show Rachel how you say hello.>

*There isn't any difference.*

<You do one when you're leaving and another when you've just arrived.> "Say goodbye, Dickens."

Looking at Su with a golden grin on his face, Dickens bowed: front feet stretched in front, chest on the ground, head up, butt up, tail wagging.

Su laughed. "That's priceless. Thank you, Dickens." Elbows touching her waist, she raised her arms, palms of her hands together, and dipped her head. "This is a Japanese 'goodbye.'"

Rachel did perk up when Dickens put his head on her pillow and softly licked her ear. *She's sad. And worried.*

I didn't want to seem pushy, but a little nudge might be okay. Sometimes our friends welcome a chance to vent.

"Rachel, is there anything I can do for you?"

"Sure," she said. "Get me a new pair of lungs before the ones I have give up completely and they move me to the care wing."

I understood what she wasn't saying. In the assisted living wing of the residence, the activity room hums. There's a spinning wheel and loom for creating yarns with the coats of llamas, alpacas, sheep, and – in one case – Malemute. Crocheters and knitters argue over possession of these donated treasures. There are also woodworking tools, painting supplies, and scrapbooking materials – something for anyone wanting to keep their hands and minds engaged.

Evergreen's dining room and sitting room serve double duty as concert halls for musician volunteers and residents who enjoy playing the piano and those who are content to listen. And there is a well-stocked library and newspaper reading room.

In the care wing are those waiting for the all-too-infrequent visitor or for some other release from boredom and despair. Residents there can't activate the code that would let them go to the activity rooms and aides are too few and usually too busy to take them there.

Rachel shook her head. "Sorry. I usually squeeze every drop of pleasure I can out of each day."

*They need more visitors like me. Everybody cheers up when I come. It works with you at home, too.*

<Yes. You are very proficient at poking your nose under my elbows so I have to stop knitting or reading.>

I thought Rachel might perk up if I could start her talking. "Rachel, you've told me about your life in the California hills and the animals you shared that life with. Did you ever have a horse?"

"Oh, yes. Lad's best friend after me was Concho, a pinto gelding that I rescued from a rodeo. German shepherds are basically herding dogs, you know, despite all the tales of them as war dogs and police dogs and guard dogs. Well, Lad had the instinct very strongly. He herded the ducks and chickens. Was not so successful with the cats or the little dogs. But he was in heaven when Concho came to live with us. He and that horse would race each other, on separate sides of the pasture fence, from one end to the other.

"One day, a sudden storm blew up over the ridge to our west. Concho was in the far pasture and I knew there wasn't time for me to coax him in. Frantic, I raced through the barn, Lad at my heels, and pointed across the field. 'Get Concho,' I said. He paused only a second to look at me and my pointing finger before flying through the pasture. I don't know what or how he communicated with the horse, but soon Lad was running back toward me, Concho right beside him. They stopped briefly at the barn door before, I swear, tiptoeing inside. Lad stopped just outside Concho's stall, waiting until his friend ambled in and I closed the gate to escort me back to the house just as the hail started."

Not long after that, Rachel moved to a hospice room. When we entered, the stench nearly made me gag.

*Friend Rachel needs a bath. She didn't get to the bathroom fast enough.*

Rachel hadn't been able to get to a bathroom by herself for several weeks, but until today, she had been changed often and bathed regularly, if only a bed bath.

She looked up at me from her nest of pillows. "I am so sorry. I know I stink. They tried to get me into the walk-in tub, but if I have to sit up straight, I can't breathe."

I couldn't believe that the staff would leave her lying in her own filth without trying to figure out a humane way to clean her up. I helped her get a drink of juice and straightened out her hat, which had slid halfway off her head. Then, telling her we'd come again the next week, I went in search of a nurse.

I was relieved to learn that everyone was as concerned as I was. A bed bath wasn't the answer; Rachel needed to soak in an Epsom salts bath. Figuring out how to accomplish that wasn't easy.

*Could she float in a pool like the kids next door have?*
<Dickens, you are a genius!>

I told the nursing director, "I know you can't put her in the swimming pool - it would have to be drained and fully sterilized - and the facility doesn't have a hot tub, but Kmart and WalMart carry cheap kids' wading pools that would be big enough to lay Rachel down in."

I don't know – because I didn't ask – if they used my idea or figured out something else, but the following week, Rachel's room smelled only of lavender. She smiled weakly and dropped a hand over the side of the bed to pet Dickens, but she couldn't sit up. She couldn't even straighten herself on her pillows without help. Her lovely face was gaunt and gray, her silver hair dull and lifeless, and her head lolled to one side, the hat askew. Once she was straightened out and the head of the bed elevated a bit, she seemed to gain some strength.

"I have to get out of here," she said. "I need to get back to my weaving and jewelry making. There are only so many people I can e-mail. I can't just lie here and stare at the ceiling all day."

When we stopped to see her the next week and the week after, she was sound asleep.

*Will you wake her up? Maybe she'll get better if she sleeps the hurt away. I always feel ready to party when I wake up from a nap.*

<Party?>

*Well, you know: go for a long walk with you, come and visit our friends, greet people at our front door. That's a party!*

A week before Christmas, Rachel was awake when we came. So thin, I could see every bone and vein in her arms. But she was propped up on her pillows, her hat was on straight, her hair was clean and shiny, and she was smiling. "My boys are coming for Christmas! Rob from California, Justin from Texas. I can hardly wait!"

# *Enid*

The obituaries for Rachel and John were in the newspaper three days after Christmas. With a heavy heart, I told Dickens we had visits to make. I wondered if any other friends had died during the holidays. We stopped first at Enid's room.

*If she offers me a cookie, I guess I can't have it. But she might have ice cubes. She did once before.*

Enid isn't really a dog person, although she would willingly share some of her cookies, pudding, and plate of left-over dinner with him. She prefers human visitors, the more the merrier. Her bed is big enough and sturdy enough for all four of her grandkids to pile on. Enid is morbidly obese, a medical phrase that refers to patients whose weight will eventually kill them. They usually have single rooms with king-size beds on heavy duty frames.

"I'm going to be with my family at Christmas," Enid had told me early in December. "My sons and son-in-law are figuring out how to get me there. They live miles from here. But we're going to do it!"

I waited to hear if her wish had become a reality.

*I'll just lie down here and snooze while you two talk. Maybe her grandkids will come while we're here. They*

**34**

*like me a lot.*

Enid thoroughly enjoyed the word picture she painted.

"We couldn't afford a forty-mile ambulance ride, but my son-in-law has a pickup truck, so all they needed to do was get me and my bed into the back of the truck. They sure couldn't just lift the bed with me in it, so they built a ramp out of left over bits of plywood and two-by-fours. It was pretty steep, and a bit too narrow, and a couple times, I nearly rolled right off, but we made it. And off we went."

*I guess she couldn't just jump in like I do.*

I had to turn around and fake a cough so Enid wouldn't hear the snort I couldn't suppress. If I tried to explain, she would probably laugh, but I might hurt her feelings. I had a vivid picture of 450-pound Enid jumping into her bed in the back of an open pickup, flying down the highway, waving at everyone else on the road. I had to ask, "Was the truck bed covered?"

"Oh, sure. Had one of those topper things. Otherwise, I'd have froze to death."

"How was the party?"

"Great. Probably the same food as here – turkey and stuffing and mashed potatoes and pie – but with family, it tastes better. I sat my bed up and they borrowed one of those wheeled trays from the home so I could be right close to the table with everyone else. And then we played a couple hands of Euchre and then they had to bring me back." Enid guffawed. "Nearly dropped me off the back of the truck when the ramp slid, but a couple of the staff guys here were ready to help, so we made it. I wasn't the only one that nearly had a heart attack."

I sent a silent 'thank you' heavenward, relieved that Enid, at least, had not only lived through the holidays, but had a wonderful time doing it.

# *Gina & Karl*

As usual, Dickens and I walked past Leon's door, not even glancing inside.

*He's a mean man. Why are some people mean? Don't they want friends?*

I had knocked on that door on our first visit, to be greeted by the furious face of an elf, pointy ears and all, glaring up at us from his wheel chair. As usual, I asked if he would like a dog visit. His answer was a spewed stream of filthy words. We never attempted to greet him after that.

There always seem to be at least one or two residents who want nothing to do with anyone. Some of those who have roommates never speak to them. However, they are the exceptions, outnumbered by the caregivers: Barb and Mary, who look after each other; Dana, who looks after ducks and lonely humans; Flo, who shares her visitors with bed-bound Donna and includes others in her shopping trips; Gina, who keeps Karl company and ensures that he doesn't fall in the shower.

*Is the treat already in your hand for Karl to give me?*

Karl is in his early to mid-forties. I mostly forget the fact that he is physically disabled, because sitting down, he is a boyish looking guy with wavy dark hair and a flirty smile. Gina looks perfectly healthy – late thirties or early forties, blue eyes, dark blond hair just starting to turn grey, and a petite figure. She suffers from MS, but has been in remission for over a year, she told me. She opened the door when I knocked. Karl was waiting in his recliner. Dickens immediately sat expectantly beside him, nosing at his hands. I handed Karl one of Dickens' treats, a pea-sized piece of his regular dog food.

*I smell a treat.* Karl moved it from his right hand to his left and then held out the right hand for Dickens to sniff. *He teases. Treat isn't in that hand.* Dickens' nose poked at the hand with the treat. *There it is!* "You found it," Karl said. "Clever boy. Here you are." *Yum!*

Routine game concluded, Dickens paused while Karl petted him, then moved to greet Gina. *Nice friend. No treat, but good ear scratches.*

On a subsequent visit, I tapped on Karl's door and hearing "Come in," led Dickens in. Gina came out of the bathroom. "He just got out of the shower," she said with a shy smile. "You'll be here next week?"

"We will," I assured her. "Tell Karl we'll see him then." She patted Dickens before returning to the bathroom and carefully closing the door.

Back in the hall, Dickens stopped before we got to Dottie's door and looked at me.

*Are they a mated pair?*

<Probably. What do you know about mated pairs?>

*That boy bulldog on our corner told me all about how*

*those puppies in his yard got there.*
<Oh.>


A few weeks later, as we approached Karl's door, we couldn't make out the words, but Gina and Karl were arguing.
*Are they fighting? Not nice.*
<With words, yes. We'll interrupt them.>
I rapped sharply on the door and the voices stopped before Karl said, "Come in." He had turned to seat himself in his recliner. Gina stood near the door. She stopped to pat Dickens' head and my shoulder as she walked by us. "I was just leaving. Please stop by my room when you get there."
*She's sad and kinda mad.*
<We'll visit her room. Maybe she needs to talk.>
Dickens moved to his usual position beside Karl's chair. The young man absent-mindedly went through the routine of teasing Dickens until the treat was revealed and then stroking him. "Gina's in a bit of a snit," he said, "but she'll get over it."
*If a snit is some of mad and more of sad, she's in more than a bit of it.*
<They'll talk to us about whatever's bothering them if they want to.>
Karl turned his TV back on, his usual signal that the visit was over, and thanked us for coming. We stopped to see the friends whose rooms were along the hall and around the corner between Karl's room and Gina's, but Dickens was not as eager as usual to linger with each

person.

I tapped on Gina's door and opened it. She was in her recliner, blowing her nose. "Come on in and stay for a minute, would you?"

*She needs me first. Then you can have your turn.*

Gina reached out her hands. "Come here, Dickens. I need a hug."

*See?*

Gina removed her glasses and leaned closer. "Do you give kisses, Dickens?"

*Would it be okay? She did ask.*

<Yes, because she asked. Never without being asked.>

Permission given, Dickens' soft tongue blessed her eyes, nose, and, when she turned her head, her earlobes.

After a few moments, Gina raised her head and put her hands on the sides of Dickens' face so she could talk to him eye to eye. "Okay, that's enough. Would you lie down while I talk to your mom?"

I waited to see if Dickens would do as she asked.

<Will you do that without expecting a treat?>

*She asked nicely.* He promptly lowered his body to the floor. *I'm a good boy, aren't I?*

<Yes, dear, you're a very good boy. When you choose to be.> I smiled at him to let him know I was teasing. He really is a very good boy, especially with his special friends.

"Can I do something for you, Gina?" I asked.

"Not really. I wanted to tell you something without Karl interrupting. For weeks now, I've been phoning the manager at the apartment complex where I used to live, asking if I could move back into my old apartment. It's on the other side of town, near most of my friends. My doctor made me come here last fall after my legs suddenly refused to work. When they rolled me down the hall in a wheelchair, I was mortified. Everyone was staring at me. I'm a lot better now. Some days I don't even need a cane. I'm ready to get out of here."

"That would be wonderful for you, if you could manage."

"Oh, yes. As I did before, I'd have someone to come in daily to help me with bathing and other personal needs and to cook a bit and clean every week. I got along fine before and I can again. The problem is, the manager hasn't returned my phone calls."

She lifted her chin resolutely. "So I've talked to the ombudsman at my church, and he's going to intervene."

Now I understood the reason for the quarrel with Karl. "And Karl isn't pleased at the prospect of your leaving here, right?"

"Right. It's okay for him to spend holidays and vacations with his family while I sit staring at these walls, but it's not okay with him for me not to be available when he wants company." Gina' eyes teared up.

Dickens raised his head. *He's making her sad and angry. Can we help?*

<We'll do what we can, but we have to respect her privacy. And Karl's.>

I took one of Gina's hands in mine. "If you both try, you can work through this."

"I told him that. And it will be weeks or even months

before I'd be able to leave. There aren't many low in-come/subsidized apartments available in this area."

I squeezed her hand gently and let go. "I'll keep my fingers crossed for you. And you can let me know every week how matters are progressing. This will work – and you'll be able to practice being patient."

She laughed. "I'm getting a lot of practice in here. Thank goodness I love to read and the library here has a good collection. People are good about bringing us boxes of their books instead of taking them to a sec-ond-hand store."

Dickens stood up and wagged his tail, reading the signs that Gina was feeling better. He pushed his muz-zle under the hands resting in her lap.

*Now we can go.*

"Yes, Dickens," Gina said, "now you can go see your other friends."

<Did she just hear what you were thinking or was that just coincidence?>

Dickens looked at me and rolled his eyes. He didn't reply.

On our next visit, Gina met us near the door as Karl emerged from the bathroom, clad only in a large towel. "I wouldn't dare take a shower without Gina to keep me steady, prevent me from falling." He laughed as if her help was a big joke.

Gina didn't meet my eyes as she handed him his cane and moved out of his way as he clumped toward the bedroom, clutching tightly to the towel. He stopped and turned around. "Got a treat for Dickens?"

I handed him a morsel of dog food from my pocket and he made a little sleight of hand show before holding out both hands. "Find the treat, Dickens." Dickens' nose poked at Karl's right hand, the one that had taken the treat. *Not there, I know. Game isn't fun today, but he's trying.*

Dickens shifted his attention to the other fist, which Karl opened to reveal the treat and let the dog take it.

Karl turned back, went into the bedroom, and closed the door. Dickens sighed. *He acts like he didn't really want to see us today.*

Gina's mouth smiled, but her eyes didn't. She leaned over to give Dickens a quick hug. "He wants someone to pick up after him, hand him a towel, listen to him complain. He doesn't want a friend. Or maybe it's just me."

*He should love the friends he's got.*

The following week, Karl muted the TV and asked,. "Did you see Gina?"

"Not yet," I said. "We'll check to see if she's in her room."

She was folding clothes and putting them away. She looked happier than she had for several weeks. "I heard from the ombudsman. He was getting nowhere with the apartment manager where I used to live and got my deposit back. Now he says he's found a really nice place in a new complex in the same neighborhood. So we'll see. I have to get out of here."

A week later, I saw an ambulance parked near the entrance, and as we entered, four EMTs wheeled a stretcher down the left hallway. Dickens seemed in a hurry to greet our friends along the other hall, but didn't want to dawdle. He pulled away from Karl's door.

*Not now. Nice lady is in trouble. Hurry!*

We zipped by several rooms before reaching Gina's. A quavery "Come in," answered my tap on the door. When I opened it, the EMTs were preparing to lift Gina onto the stretcher.

*She's real sick. They're taking her away. Can we visit her someplace else?*

<I'll find out. They're probably taking her to the hospital.>

It took me a while to locate Patsy, the activities director. Gina had contracted a very bad cold, which played havoc with her MS.  In addition to having trouble breathing, she had lost the ability to move her legs.

By the time I could determine which hospital she'd been taken to, she was no longer there. "She's been transferred," I was told." You might try one of the rehab places."

*Is she lost?*

<Well, I'm sure she knows where she is, but I haven't found her yet. We'll keep looking.>

She wasn't at the Center Health and Rehabilitation Center nor the Colorado Rehabilitation Hospital and I didn't know where else to look. However, as we entered Evergreen for our next visit, Dickens cheerfully greeted Don and the other staff members in the physical therapy gym and lingered to put his head in the laps of the friends using the equipment. But as we left the gym and headed toward the rooms of the other therapy patients, he picked up the pace.

His leash was taut as we approached the last room across from the lounge area. The door was open and he entered with his tail whipping in joy.

*Look who's here! We found her!*

Gina sat in a recliner, leaning forward to hug her canine friend. She didn't bother to remove her glasses as Dickens thoroughly washed them along with the rest of her face. I'd never hear Gina laugh before. "Does he do this with everyone?'

I explained that licking was discouraged and that only one other friend got the doggy kisses. "He knows he's not to lick unless someone specifically asks for it. Even with me, he does only a quick touch on an earlobe."

When we all calmed down, Gina explained how she'd come to be here. "I was in the hospital for three or four days while the antibiotics did their job. But even with the cold under control, my legs were too weak for me to move safely from bed to wheelchair, never mind to an ordinary chair. So they sent me back here, in a different room, and the physical therapy is working wonders. You should see me on that stationary bike – Tour de France, here I come!"

*She's going on a tour? Where's France?*

"Will you go back to your old room when you're ready?" I asked.

"Oh, no. And that's the best thing ever. All the papers are signed, I've made the deposit, and I'll be moving into my new apartment in a couple weeks. It's real close to where I used to live, and all my old friends have rallied around and are busy moving my furniture and other stuff in. When I get there, we'll have a party. You and Dickens will come, won't you?"

*A party! I love parties. Will there be ice cubes? And maybe peanut butter stuffed celery?*

<If we go, you are NOT allowed to beg celery from people.>

*What if it accidentally falls on the floor?*

# *Dottie*

Dottie is a tiny, spry woman who usually wears a twinkling smile, although her life has not been easy. We were talking one day about the world situation, and Dottie volunteered the information that she was living in Pearl Harbor on December 7, 1941. "I still have nightmares about the noise and the fires and my parents crying. As soon as it was safe to leave, my mom, my sisters, and I were sent to live with relatives in Pennsylvania. We worried about Dad and all our friends back in Hawaii. We got letters, whole batches of them, about once a month. Right after the battle of Midway, Dad decided we should come home. Flying over the harbor, we all cried. We could see some of the destroyed ships lying on the bottom of the ocean near the shore." Momentarily, Dottie's smile disappeared and her eyes focused on something long ago and far away. "But we won, didn't we?"

*Why is she so sad?*

<Sometimes people remember long ago events that they can never forget.>

*We dogs remember some stuff, mostly really super or really awful. But we forget a lot, too. Like why my eating rabbit poop makes you so cross.*

# Dickens' Friends

*I know what makes Dottie happy – besides my cuddles of course. She likes to sit with her legs crossed moving bits of paper around on a big board.*

<She does jigsaw puzzles. They're cardboard pictures that have been cut into different shapes. People find it restful to put the pieces back together>

*Beth plays with pieces of cardboard, too. On a card table. She dropped a piece on the floor once and I picked it up to see how it tasted. She nicely told me to 'Give it.' So I did. And she said, "Thank you, Dickens." She always says my name when she's talking to me. Most of our friends do. Even Valerie remembers my name most of the time. And it's okay if she forgets a little bit and calls me Dinkums.*

<I try to use people's names when I talk to them. They don't really like being called "dear" or "honey." It seems as if people who do that can't be bothered to remember them as individuals.>

*Some don't know your name, but they like you anyway.*

<They know who I am: the lady at the end of your leash.>

*We couldn't be here if you didn't hold my leash. I think that's one of the rules. Like how Dottie used to have to go outside, cuz that's where all the smokers have to go. But then she quit. Maybe if Big John had quit, he'd still be here.*

Dottie missed John when his years of rough living caught up with him and he lost his will to live. "We were good friends. Once he found out I used to drive

**48**

the big rigs, I'm not sure which of us told the taller tales."

*I miss Big John, too. I don't like it when friends go away.*

Thinking of friends who'd gone away, I asked Dottie if she'd heard from Gina since she moved into her new apartment.

Dottie brightened up. "I not only heard from her, Skip — you know Skip, the helping guy from church —anyway, Skip drove me over to Gina's new place. She's so happy, and she's doing real good.

"And, best news ever, Skip's looking for a place for me, too. Since I quit smoking, I'm pretty healthy, and the doc says I don't have to stay here. So I just need to find a place of my own. But I'll be here a while yet, and I'll always look forward to your visits."

*Will all our friends go away?* Dickens sighed and his tail and ears drooped the minute we were back in the hall.

<If they can, yes.>

His tail drooped lower.

<Dickens, do you remember when I got hurt and friends brought you to visit me in a place like this? It wasn't my real home; it was a special place like this where there are people  like our friends Diane, Katy, and Chelsea, specially trained to look after folks who are sick or hurt. Almost everyone here wants to go back to their real home.>

*Did Big John?*

<Probably not. For some people, this is their real

home. Their kind of sick is not ever going to get better, so they always need special care,>

*So Dottie will be really happy when she can go away from here. If she will be happy, I will be happy.* The plume of his tail once again was carried high and was waving.

# Rehab

The next time we saw Gina, she was in the therapy gym, pumping vigorously on one of the stationary bikes. She grinned and waved, saying, "I'm moving to-morrow! Can I talk to Dickens in a few minutes, after I'm finished here?"

That was fine with Dickens and me; several others were waiting to take a breather from their exercises and to visit for a few minutes.

Until I was a therapy patient myself, I didn't fully re-alize how necessary visitors are, especially canine visi-tors. I spent ten days at Evergreen after my knees were replaced. Good friends Lisa and Brat, another therapy dog team, paid me a visit. Brat, all seven pounds of her, happily curled up on the bed beside me, thoroughly en-joying the cuddle we shared. When Lisa reached down to pick the dog up, ready to leave, Brat spun her head toward her mistress, bared her teeth and growled. Her message couldn't have been clearer: *I'm not ready to leave.*

We still laugh about that moment, but anyone who ever thought that humans are the bosses and dogs are their slaves never heard of partnerships.

We don't usually get to know the patients in the therapy room very well, since they aren't long term residents. But they enjoy taking a break from often painful exercises, and Dickens and I love meeting new people.

On occasion, we see friends from the outside world. Bobbie had suffered a mild stroke from which no one doubted she'd fully recover. Her name was on the prayer list at church so everyone was praying for her, not just friends like me who served on Altar Guild with her. Dickens and I found her hooked up to a machine designed to strengthen arm muscles. "It looks like you're quickly regaining the use of that left arm," I said. "How's the leg?"

*I know her! She's been at that place where everyone prays a lot and you sometimes take me when you go for meetings. And I got blessed that one time when a bunch of us dogs and a couple cats got special attention.*

Bobbie greeted Dickens first, stroking under his chin and then rubbing behind his ears. "I'm doing very well," she said. "Better than the doctor thought I would at this point. I've been here three weeks now and may be able to go home next week. I'll miss your visits. For everyone here, they are bright spots in otherwise sometimes tedious days."

I thanked her. "If you're not here next week, I'll look forward to seeing you back in church."

We'd seen Don every week for months, but not as a patient. He was one of the physical therapists at Evergreen, especially popular with the ladies, since he had curly brown hair, a nice build, and twinkly eyes. He was young enough to be the son or grandson of many of his charges, and they doted on him. Yet here he was, wearing a cast from right ankle to thigh. He grinned wryly and answered my question before I asked: "I should make up a good story, like maybe I was doing a routine on my snowboard and came down wrong, but the truth is I tripped over my son's tricycle and broke my tibia."

While Don was talking, Dickens laid his head in his friend's lap and listened intently, his eyes never leaving Don's face. He cocked his ears as if he was puzzled. *He thinks this is funny. Getting hurt isn't funny, is it? Or is it funny that he now has to do what he used to tell others to do? People are so complicated.*

Roberto was waiting for a kidney transplant. One of his twice weekly dialysis treatments is done the morning of the day we visit. Once in a while, he is sound asleep, exhausted by the treatment, but usually he is bright and perky, glad to see friends, human or canine. When he's feeling really good, he can be found in the therapy room, keeping his leg muscles strong by pumping away at the stationary bike for half an hour or more and then using the arm stretching machine.

Valerie spends most of her time in the therapy room, but not exercising. That room and the adjoining lounge are her social center, where she reads the paper, does the crossword puzzle, and chats with anyone willing to talk and listen. She surprised me one day by stating that although Don thought she hung out in the therapy room because she had a crush on him, she didn't trust him. "He's too cute, and he knows it."

*She's old enough to be Don's grandmother! She's nice, and she loves me, and most of the time she remembers my name, but she isn't young and pretty. She's got more wrinkles than you do.*

<She doesn't see herself that way. She remembers when she was young and pretty and had a loving husband and children. Her memories are happy ones and maybe it's a blessing that she doesn't always remember yesterday or last week.>

*Oh. Well, I love her and Don flirts with her and everyone else, so I guess it's okay.*

And then there was Tom. A good-looking young man – really young, maybe thirty – waved us over to the mat where he was doing leg lifts. "Hi! I'm Tom and this must be Dickens." He grinned. "No one seemed to remember your name, but they all assured me that 'the lady who holds Dickens' leash is real nice.'"

*Don't feel bad that some people don't know your name. You are real nice. Maybe it's because they can't pet you.*

I laughed. "Hi, Tom. Yes, I know Dickens is the star. I'm Judie, the leash lady." I glanced at his bare knees and recognized the scars. "I see you're recovering from double knee replacements. Who's your surgeon?"

He told me and I nodded. "He's one of the best, and

about the only one that will do both knees at once. Good luck with the rehab."

"Thanks. I'd better get back to work. Maybe when you come next week I'll be up and walking."

The next week, he was not up and walking. He was lying in bed, his eyes full of pain, but with a brave smile. His right leg was in a cast from ankle to groin.

"What happened? I asked.

Tom shrugged. "Both knees were coming along nicely. But I'm an independent cuss and I thought I could get into my friend's car by myself. Slipped on the ice and broke the leg in two places." He laughed. "The knee was fine. Above it and below, not so much. So here I am, needing a few weeks of therapy."

Dickens put his head on Tom's pillow, sighed, and stared at him.

"If I didn't know better, I'd say your dog just told me to work real hard in the rehab room, do everything the therapists tell me, and I'll be all better."

*It's good when people listen to me.*

Tom looked at Dickens, then at me. "Could he have a treat?" I usually say no, that my dog works for love and the occasional ice cube, but I could see Tom really wanted to give him something, so I said, "His digestive system is very sensitive, but a few kinds of treats are fine."

"Peanut butter?"

*Peanut butter! Oh, wow! Oh, yes! Oh, please!*

Tom pulled his wheeled tray table closer and reached for a jar. He turned the top toward me so I could read the magic marker words: "Only for dogs, not people."

He grinned and I laughed as he unscrewed the lid and scooped out a teaspoonful with his finger. He told Dickens to sit and then let him lick off every bit, even under the fingernail.

I pretended to disapprove. "You do know what you've started?"

"Sure. It's a good way to keep him coming back. And when they turn me loose from here, I'll have someone else serve as keeper of the peanut butter."

At our next visit to Evergreen, Tom wasn't in the therapy room and he wasn't in his room. I asked one of the nurses if he had been discharged. "No. I guess you hadn't heard. He was doing really well – you know, you've seen him pushing himself to regain his strength and mobility. Anyway, a really virulent infection set in to his right knee, and Tom lost the leg. He'll be in the rehabilitation hospital for the next few weeks, learning to use a prosthesis. He talked to Don: as soon as he can, he wants to come back here for advanced therapy once he's on his feet again – so to speak."

Tom was back several weeks later, big grin on his face, delighted to see Dickens, and eager to show off his new leg, the wildest bit of psychedelic art I have ever seen outside an art gallery. It's orange, purple, yellow, green, red, and blue in a swirl of eye-popping color from mid-thigh to ankle. I doubt that anything will ever slow this man down.

Dickens sniffed the leg, looked up at Tom, and gave him his golden grin. *I get that it's substituting for a real bone. I wouldn't bite Tom's real leg, and I won't bite this. But I do wonder what it would taste like. Probably not peanut butter.*

Tom wasn't in the therapy room the following week. We met him moving briskly up the hall with the help of just a cane. "Look at you go!" I said. He grinned and waved his cane in the air.

*He's almost all better, isn't he? I remember when he couldn't hardly get himself out of bed.* The tail drooped a bit. *I guess he'll be leaving soon. No more peanut butter?*

Dickens needn't have worried. The peanut butter jar was now in the top drawer of Jason's dresser.

# *Adult Day Care Center*

*This place is different, but I like it. In a different way, you know?*

<Different how?>

*Well, when we go to that other place there's some-times lots of friends in one of the party rooms. But mostly we find them alone in their rooms.*

<That's true. Sometimes they prefer not to spend too much time with the other residents. They like to read or watch TV or take naps.>

*This place isn't like that. They all sit around the room in their chairs, and we don't get to spend as much time with each one as I'd like to, 'cuz everyone wants a turn to touch me and talk to me. Sometimes they fall asleep in their chairs, like you do sometimes. Don't they have beds?*

<No, because they don't live here. They come during the day when their families are at work, to be with other people and have lunch, listen to stories, have concerts and sing-a-longs, make things like Christmas decora-tions, and have visitors like us.>

*Don't our friends in those other places have families to live with?*

<Some don't. Others are so sick they need nurses

available all day and all night, but their families and friends visit. Others never have visitors.>

*They have us.*

Gwen was always delighted to have us chat for a few moments every Wednesday. She had a caring family that included a much loved dog, but at ninety years old and frail, she couldn't be left alone. Her daughter and son-in-law worked and their children were adults with their own jobs and families, too far away to visit except at Christmas. Gwen spent weekdays at the adult day care center where snacks, lunch, activities, and companionship were available.

"You are such a bonny, sweet, well-behaved dog," Gwen told Dickens as she stroked the sides of his face and gradually moved her care-worn hands to massage his ears and neck.

*If I were a cat, I'd purr. Not that I would ever want to be a cat, you know. They don't get to go for walks and visit friends and run around the park.*

"Dickens is bigger than my Albert, but about the same color. Albert's a Norfolk terrier, and if you know terriers, they are not always very well behaved."

*I do have nice manners, don't I?*

Gwen's manners and her soft accent prompted me to ask where in England she grew up.

"I was born and raised in York. Lovely old city, one of the three remaining walled cities in England, far prettier than the other two, if I do say so myself. The sloping sides of the long dried up moat wear tiers of daffodils in the spring"

*My yard has daffodils, but our city isn't called York, is it? Any connection to Yorkies like my friend Thunder?*

<Yes, actually. Yorkshire terriers originated in England, near the city of York.>

Gwen continued. "Someone long ago had the wit to ban buildings within a hundred yards of the outer walls of the city, so the moat is a sea of yellow in the spring, lush green in autumn and pristine white in winter – if we get snow. Some years we don't."

Karen, sitting next to Gwen, demanded her turn with the dog, so we moved on, Dickens wagging his tail and turning his head to look at Gwen. *We'll be back.*

Several weeks later, after our usual chat about places in the British Isles both Gwen and I were familiar with, I asked how she happened to come to Colorado.

"When I was shipped back home from Burma at the end of the war, I started off in a hospital ship bound for San Diego. There were a lot of wounded Yanks on board to look after."

*Are Yanks like Yorkies?*

<No, dear. English people often refer to Americans like me as Yanks.>

*And me? Am I a Yank?*

<No, the word only applies to people.>

*Oh. Did she just say she married one?*

She had said that and added, "I didn't get back to England for fifteen years, and then only to visit my family and finally let them meet my children."

We would have continued our chat, but every other Wednesday at two o'clock, a volunteer group of musicians comes in to lead a sing-a-long, so it was time for Dickens and me to leave.

"I want to hear more," I said. "But I don't sing very well and although Dickens has a lovely yodel, it is loud. We'll come next week with more questions."

*I like to sing along when you're in the shower, but I guess we aren't as good as these special visitors. I'll just wave a paw at them to say goodbye.*

We resumed our conversation a week later. "Gwen, you said you were in Burma at the end of the war? Why?" I asked.

Gwen sat up straight and said with a proud smile, "I was one of Queen Alexandra's nurses. Not her personally, of course. She established a special group of skilled nurses during the first war and the government has kept it going ever since."

I could picture Gwen as a young woman, barely out of her teens. Her skin, though creased with laugh lines and worry lines, was unblemished and the fine bones of her face still hinted at the lovely English rose she must have been. I smiled as she continued her story.

"Twenty or thirty of us, all recently finished with school, joined up in 1943. We endured rigorous training for several months and sailed across the Pacific in time to set up field hospitals to care for fellow Brits and a few Yanks who'd been rescued from Japanese prison camps or injured in recent fighting."

I told Gwen that I had read a bit about the conditions in those makeshift hospitals: debilitating heat and humidity, nasty bugs, brazen rats, and the occasional poisonous snake making an already difficult job nearly impossible.

Gwen shrugged at those distractions. "It was the smells: gangrene, mildew, blood and other bodily fluids, and the pervading odor of bleach and other disinfectants that were never strong enough."

Even just hearing about the odors triggered my gag reflex. Dickens cocked his ears and looked at me. *I don't get why you humans are so upset by the smell of blood and other body stuff, even bad breath. We dogs can tell right away if a creature is sick, just by how it smells.*

Dickens was right. Research suggests that some dogs sense illnesses like cancer and diabetes. Specialized service dogs have proven their ability to detect convulsions, hypoglycemia, and other events in time to give warning.

I patted his shoulder. <Your sniffer is lots keener than mine. Good thing for us both.>

I've often wondered how doctors and nurses cope with the odors they have to deal with – or ignore. "Gwen," I asked, "how could you bear it?"

She leaned over to take Dickens' head between her hands and look into his eyes. "There were dogs. Did I tell you about the dogs?"

*I want to know about the dogs. Were they like me? Did they love everybody and make them feel better? We dogs are good at that.*

It required little urging for Gwen to tell us more. "I suspect every military base, camp, or field hospital has at least a couple dogs, giving boys something to live for, as Dickens does when he visits us; radiating love and concern. Our dogs would lie down next to wounded boys, careful not to bump them. They'd stand by a bed as long as a hand rested on their neck or shoulders, mourning every death, rejoicing in every recovery. They invited the more able-bodied boys to play."

*I know how to do that. I stretch my front paws out in front, my head on the ground, my back legs holding my butt in the air, and my tail wagging. And I grin. See?*

I asked, "Where did the dogs come from?"

"We never really knew, of course, but they acted like they'd once had their own boys, and I think they needed our patients – and us, of course – to be their new families."

*Were they lost dogs? I'm glad they got found.*

Gwen wasn't there the next time we visited. Her son-in-law had been promoted and transferred to Ohio, and her daughter had retired to stay at home with her mom.

I wanted to know more about Gwen's life, but sometimes our friends' stories are left unfinished.

The first time we met Carol, she showed us the picture of her dog. Dickens doesn't usually show any interest in photographs, but this time, he wagged his tail and started panting. *I know that girl! That's Sadie from the end of our block.*

"What's your dog getting so excited about?" Carol asked.

"Dickens is looking at that picture and thinks he's seeing a Cairn terrier from our neighborhood."

"Ah, no, Dickens," she said, coaxing him to sit in front of her. "Tia and I were best friends many, many years ago. She's gone now."

"But she'll be waiting for you at the Rainbow Bridge," I said.

"What's that?"

*Tell her the story.*

"Well, according to the story, there's a bridge this side of heaven with a huge meadow in front of it. Our beloved four-footed companions wait there for us, no longer old, no longer hurting. When we get there, they cross the bridge into heaven with us."

Carol thought about that for a minute, then laughed. "That's wonderful. It really gives a good reason for welcoming the end when it comes, and not being afraid. Thank you."

I learned later that Carol had suffered a series of mini strokes. A month after we met, a major one took her life.

*Gone. But Tia was there, so it's okay.*

We chatted with Hank at the center every week for nearly two years. Each time, his face lit up when he saw Dickens and the two of them enjoyed their mutual hugs. We heard about Hank's dog, "about the size of this nice boy. His name was Rover, and he was what they call a farm collie. I loved him. He's been gone a long time."

*Gone. That's sad. But I remind Hank of his lost dog. Not lost, really. Just gone. To that bridge? So he'll be there waiting when Hank goes?*

<Yes, dear, he will.>

One week Hank wasn't at day care, but family members sometimes have days off, so I assumed he was at home. When he wasn't there the next week or the week after, I asked where he was, and was told he'd had a heart attack. He was in hospice care at Evergreen Manor.

Dickens and I hurried down the corridor. Hank had never looked robust, but on prior visits, his wiry frame looked strong, his color was good, and his smile was joyful. If he hadn't smiled, I wouldn't have recognized the frail figure lying in a hospital bed, looking every day of his ninety two years.

*Kisses?*

<I think he'd like that.>

Hank had moved his head and shoulders closer to the edge of the bed, so his face was within tongue reach. The smile grew broader and more joyful and he shut his eyes as Dickens gave gentle doggy kisses from ear to ear and forehead to chin.

We'd never talked much about Hank's life. Now that we had him all to ourselves, I started asking questions: Where did he grow up? Did he have siblings? Was he in the armed forces during WWII? When did he come to Colorado?

"I was the middle one. Three older brothers, three younger ones. We lived on a farm in Iowa. Worked really hard, but we also played really hard. You ever had the chance to play in a haystack? I can still see us, making footholds on one side of the big stack, bigger than our house, and climbing up carefully so's not to have it all come down on us, and then playing King of the Hill when we got to the top. You done that? You stand up there, by yourself for a minute, spread your arms as if you could fly, and holler, "I'm the king of the hill!" And then one of your brothers gives you a shove and down you go, feet first or face first, better than any playground slide ever imagined. And when you get your breath back, you run around to the other side, climb up again, and do it all over.

"We taught Rover – that was our dog – I told you about him, didn't I? About the same size as your guy and the same color. God, we loved that dog."

*That's why he likes me so much! Can we play on a haystack some time?*

"Anyway, we taught Rover to climb the haystack without sliding off and pulling down enough hay to bury himself. The first time, we had to give him a little shove, but after that, he'd plant his butt and his front feet, push off with his back feet, and go sailing down, just like a little kid on a snow sled."

One of the nurses came in as Hank was finishing his story, so Dickens and I left, assuring our friend that we'd be back to hear his war stories. I hoped he would still be there.

# Dickens' Friends

*He's not ready to go yet. He'll be waiting for us.*

He was. He picked up the story from where he'd left off. "I told you about the haystack when I was a kid? Well, the only war story I've ever told – or ever want to tell – also involved a haystack. Someplace in the middle of France.

"My buddies and I figured we were at least a couple miles from the German lines, and it was one of those rare, quiet, sunny days and we were in a field that somehow had escaped being bombed or burned. And there was a haystack. Not all of the guys grew up on farms, but four or five of us did, and we couldn't resist. We were on top of that pile within minutes. Soon most of the rest of the guys were up there with us. I don't know who was the first one to shout, 'I'm king of the hill!' but he wasn't the last. Most of us had already slipped joyously down the stack when we saw company coming. Krauts. We froze. Our rifles were too far away to reach; we'd be dead before we could get halfway to them."

*I wasn't even there and I'm scared! But he's still here, so things must have turned out okay.*

"So what did you do?" I asked.

"Like I said, we froze. And watched with our jaws dropping as those German boys put their guns down in a pile not too far from ours, took off their helmets, and hesitantly started walking toward us. One boy, evidently the leader, called out in pretty good English, 'May we join you?'

"One of our guys, Swede, I think, poked me. I guess I was elected spokesman. 'You want to climb the hay?'"

"'Jawohl. We like Koenig auf das Berg, what you call King of the Hill.'

"They were just boys. We were just boys. And for an hour one day in the middle of a terrible war, we all played together as boys will."

*I like boys. Some of them when they grow up still act like boys. I love it when grown up cousin Chris rolls around with me on the floor. I don't suppose Hank can roll on the floor anymore, but I think he'd like to.*

"That's a wonderful story, Hank. I hope you have more tales to tell when we come next week. Meanwhile, get well. You're in my prayers."

All of our special friends are in my prayers, but for those in hospice care, I usually pray for strength, comfort, and, if healing is no longer possible, a gentle death.

Hank wasn't in his room the next week. Family members were celebrating his birthday with him in one of the lounge areas. A week later, he was sound asleep, so I simply made sure he was breathing. The week after that, as usual, Dickens and I visited the day care center two days before our Friday visit to Evergreen.

And there, sitting in his usual recliner, was Hank. Dickens padded quickly past two other friends and, tail wagging furiously, put his head in Hank's lap. After a lovely long love fest, Dickens backed up and Hank stood up to give me a hug and whispered, "I guess your prayers worked."

# *Dana*

<Let's go see if Dana's in her room.>
*The duck lady?*
Dana is the keeper of the ducks. For the past several springs, two mama ducks have chosen to lay their eggs and hatch their ducklings in one of Evergreen's patios. Tall stone walls protect the area from intruders, including the ubiquitous geese that waddle all over the surrounding yards and open spaces, leaving piles of poop wherever they go.

Although there are large ponds in the park across the street, there are also geese, so the mother ducks choose safety, undisturbed food, and human aid over more suitable surroundings.

Almost before I tapped on her door, Dana came out of her bedroom with a huge grin on her face and hands gesturing as if sign language was needed to supplement English. "The ducklings have hatched!"

For the next several weeks, Dana told us, she and two or three others she could coax into helping would set their alarms for 5:30, carry large bags of the proper mixture of grains out to the patio, dump the dirty water from the plastic kiddie wading pool that served in lieu of a proper pond, and refill it with fresh water.

# Dickens' Friends

Every day, at noon and late afternoon, Dana and the others would repeat their chores, thanked only by the tiny quacks of the ducklings, who would persist in clustering around the feet of their nursemaids.

Dana is one of those very tall women who carries her height proudly. She is also quite lovely: salt and pepper hair casually held in a clasp at the back of her neck, classic features in a virtually unlined face. For several weeks, I guessed she was in her early forties. On one visit, we met her younger daughter, who was celebrating her fortieth birthday by taking her mom out for lunch. I added twenty years to my estimate of Dana's age.

"Have you seen Mom's ducks?" the daughter asked. I assured her that we had seen them and heard all about Dana's job as their foster mother.

Dana is a caregiver, not only for ducks. She takes under her wing new residents, who are often confused, bewildered, and feeling abandoned. She introduces them to others and helps them settle in. Dickens recognized a kindred soul the moment they met, although it took a while before he fully understood how ducks fit into her life.

*Duck tastes funny.*
<When did you ever taste duck?>
*I retrieved the baby one that tried to fly.*
<Oh, that one. It was a young robin, not a duck.>
*Robin, duck – they're both birds.*
<True. Maybe they all taste the same.>
Dana looked at Dickens, then at me. "Are you two

carrying on a non-verbal conversation?" She didn't sound surprised.

"Yes, we do that sometimes," I admitted. "We didn't mean to be rude."

She laughed. "It's okay. My cat and I used to do that. It bugged my sister. What were you talking about, if I may ask?"

I recapped the thought exchange. Dickens bumped my leg with his head. *Tell her I don't eat the babies I save.*

"Don't get the wrong idea, please, Dana. Dickens didn't eat the fledgling robin. After trying to fly from the top of our garden fence to the other side, it crash landed on the lawn. Dickens picked it up and came to me, trying unsuccessfully to spit it out. I carefully pried open his mouth and there it was, sitting on his tongue, surrounded by the cage of his teeth. He let me lift it out and watched as I set it on the other side of the fence at the base of a lilac bush."

I laughed, rubbed Dickens' head, and said. "You aren't the only bird rescuer, Dana"

*But does she also rescue baby rabbits?*

At our next visit, Dana looked awful: dark circles under her eyes and the limp posture of someone needing a long nap. But her smile lit up the area. "Another week and they'll be ready to go to the big pond."

*She's really happy! And really tired.* Dickens' tail moved like the baton of a conductor well into "The Stars and Stripes Forever." Dana leaned over to greet him, stroking his head and shoulders.

She bubbled about how much the ducklings had grown (and how much they were eating.) There are times when Dana is so weak she can't get out of bed, so it's lovely to see her so happy and so apparently healthy. For her, duck therapy works.

Dana didn't wait for a tap on her door the next time we came. She stood in the living room area of the little suite, drooping with fatigue but with dancing eyes and a huge smile. "We did it! The ducklings and their mamas are safely across the street in the big pond, euphorically paddling their little hearts out."

*And nobody told me! I could've helped.*

"Tell us all about it," I asked Dana.

"Skip and I and two or three others – Su was there and I think Jim and Mike – filled our hands and pockets with corn kernels and grain and got as close as we dared to the mother ducks before dropping bits of food as we walked toward the gate. Sharon opened it right before we started the trek."

*If I'd been here, I could've brought up the rear. Herding them, you know.*

<You're a retriever, not a herding dog.>

*I know all about it. I've watched Baxter herd human kids.*

"So the mother ducks followed the trail of crumbs and the ducklings followed the moms?" I asked.

"Exactly! You'd have laughed – we did – at the parade of two mama ducks followed by twenty-one ducklings in a double line all the way across the patio and through the gate."

Dana's hands waved like a traffic cop's, unconsciously repeating the gestures she'd used to keep her flock moving.

"And none of them tried to go back to the patio?"

Dana shook her head. "We anticipated that and Sharon closed the gate as soon as we thought the last one was through. Jim and Mike hurried ahead to stop traffic and Skip and I kept laying down a trail of treats. It took at least ten minutes, but as soon as the mother ducks scented the pond, they waddled as fast as they could and splooshed in, swimming a couple tight circles before turning to coax their babies into the water."

"Wait a minute," I said. "You said twenty-one ducklings. I thought there were twenty-two."

Dana laughed. "It wasn't funny at the time, but it is now. One stubborn little creature hid behind a bush in the patio and was shut in when Sharon closed the gate. As soon as we got back to start cleaning up the area, we heard it peeping piteously. But did he let us pick him up and take him to his mother and siblings? Oh, no. We chased that little turkey around and around for ages."

*What turkey? I thought we were talking about ducks. And now I know I should have been there. I'd have retrieved that peeper really fast.*

"Finally, Jim took off his shirt and threw it on top of the little one and before it could escape, picked it up and wrapped the shirt around the squirming baby. He thrust it at me. 'Here, you carry it across the street. I'd probably drop it right in front of a car.'

"So back across the street I went. By now one of the mother ducks had counted her brood and realized she was a duckling short. She was quacking frantically, her other babies were swimming in circles and cheeping in distress, and the other duck family was swimming to the other side of the pond to get away from the racket. I set the duckling on the ground and quickly loosened his impromptu robe. The reunion was heartwarming." Dana's eyes filled up as she remembered the finale of the duckling adventure.

"Maybe we should have phoned and asked you and Dickens to help."

*I said that. We'd have got the job done in half the time.*

<Maybe. Or you might have scared the mother ducks into flying and putting all the ducklings into a panic.>

*Yeah, I guess. Ducks are awful flighty, aren't they?*

# *Su*

Although she and Rachel were roommates before Rachel's condition became critical, Dickens and I didn't know Su well. The day we first met her, she sat patiently in a recliner, John Grisham's *The Painted House* open on her lap. Dickens sat down in front of her, politely waiting for her to close the book.

"Well aren't you a lovely big boy?"

*Yes, I am.*

"See that picture over there of the Chihuahua? My Taco was just a tiny thing, but he had a Napoleon complex – thought he was big enough to take on a rhinocerous or anything else that looked like a challenge. Come closer, Dickens, if you want your ears scratched."

As she fondled the dog, we talked about books. Like me, she liked mysteries, adventure tales, but admitted to a sneaking fondness for Regency romance novels.

"Books help the days pass. And I take a walk every day. They don't like us walking too far, where they can't see us. Some people in here have trouble remembering where they are, but I'm not senile. Not yet, anyway. I can find my way back, and I learned how to safely cross a street before I was old enough for school. Don't like being treated like a child."

That was the longest conversation we had for several months. Su was always polite, but seemed to prefer her own company. One day, however, she needed a friend.

We came through the main door to see Sharon, the facilities manager, shaking a finger at Su and scolding. I couldn't avoid overhearing. "Su, you must have a staff member with you if you intend to go around the block."

Dickens looked at me, sad-eyed, tugging slightly at his leash. *Our friend is sad. She doesn't know what she did wrong. Can we go comfort her?*

<In a minute. Just wait.>

Scolding over, Sharon strode back to her office.

*Now?*

We walked over to Su. "Can we walk back to your room with you?"

She nodded, head down, too proud to weep, too embarrassed to stop the errant tears.

"Why was Sharon so cross?" she asked.

"I think she was just worried about you. Francine walked too far last week and couldn't remember how to get back. Sharon was afraid you might get lost." I suggested.

"Rubbish," she muttered, just loud enough to be heard.

To take her mind off the recent mortification, I said, "Su, what did you do before you retired?"

She smiled and her eyes took on the faraway look of memory. "For many years I lived in Japan and worked as a librarian for a multinational corporation. I loved the country; I adored the people. So kind. So gentle.

So polite. I commented more than once on the impeccable manners of even the smallest children. 'Oh, no,' I was told, 'it is you Americans who show wonderful manners.'

"I'd seen how some of my compatriots behaved. So rude," she said. I didn't have to be a mind reader to know that she was still thinking of Sharon.

Dickens was looking intently at Su's bookshelves. *Look! She had another dog. One like Konrad.* I glanced that way and saw the picture: a German shepherd posed like a statue on top of a huge rock.

"Beautiful dog," I said. "What's his name?"

"That's my King," she replied. "We spent hours hiking and rock climbing. King played his own version of king of the castle. I'd be hiking along a path at the foot of the rocky foothills; he'd be pacing along with me, but at the top of the rocks. If he saw anyone approaching, he'd scramble down to guard me; as soon as we were alone again, back up he'd go." She smiled, remembering days when she was not trapped in a weakening body, in a place where the only dog she could talk to came but once a week and stayed for only a few minutes.

"King let me lean on him whenever I fell down. And I fell a lot, but never broke anything. And never when I was mountain climbing."

"Where did you go mountain climbing? Here in Colorado?"

"Some, but mostly in Japan. I climbed Mt. Fuji several times. Once I had a friend with me who was not used to high altitudes. He passed out before we reached the top, or at least the place where there was shelter and food and a terrific lookout."

"What did you do?"

"I kept going to the top, to get help. I couldn't drag him all the way, at least not fast enough. The wonderful couple who operate the shelter picked up a stretcher and followed me back to where my friend lay unconscious. Soon they had him on a cot in the shelter, wrapped in blankets. They graciously provided me with tea and cookies while they ministered to him. He came to fairly quickly, very embarrassed, but they were so kind, assuring him that he was not the first who had to be rescued and would not be the last. Tea and cookies revived him as well as me, and we got back down Mt. Fuji without further alarm. I climbed that mountain many more times. He never tried it again."

"You would enjoy hiking with me, wouldn't you Dickens?" she asked. He wagged his tail and softly touched the tip of his tongue to her hand.

# Lori and Jason

When we got home, I picked up the camera and went out the back door with Dickens. He was ready to run off some steam. His job is emotionally tiring, but not physically so, since he is required to walk slowly, sit still, and sometimes lie down and listen while others talk. Many of our friends comment on how docile he is, some even asking, "Is he always this calm?"

I wanted to take some pictures of the other Dickens, the at home Dickens, the whirling dervish Dickens to show Lori and Jason, a very attractive couple who obviously dote on each other.

Lori's cap of wavy hair is silver, her complexion clear with just a few laugh lines. Jason has a full head of pale hair, lively eyes, and a boyish face that frequently lights up with a smile. Although he is either sitting in his wheelchair or lying on the bed when we come, I can tell that unlike tiny Lori, he is tall, probably over six feet.

When I first met Lori and Jason, I assumed they were in their early seventies. Then I noticed the poster on the door, showing photos of a group of WWII sailors. One of the men was a very young Jason. WWII ended in 1945, so Jason had to be in his late eighties.

I had to ask, "How long have you two been married?"
Proudly, in unison, they replied, "Sixty nine years."
"Do you have children?"
Lori said, "Two boys and a girl. And four grandchildren, but no great grandkids yet."
Dickens rolled his eyes at me. *We have lots of grandkids, don't we? I think they're all great.*

When we visit Lori and Jason, Dickens carefully divides his time between them. He sits quietly at Lori's feet while she gets out the peanut butter jar and scoops out a blob with her index finger. She holds it out; Dickens carefully licks off every bit. Then he moves over to Jason's wheelchair and puts his head in his friend's lap as his neck and shoulders get a massage. The last time we were there, Jason said, "Look, Lori, he's going to sleep."
*Not sleeping. Enjoying the touch. Feels even better with eyes closed.*
Lori smiled. "Such a calm, gentle dog."
Yes, he is that at home – when he's asleep. Since Lori and Jason can't come to our house to meet Dickens Doufus Dog, I decided to take them some photos. The performance started with him bowing, butt in the air, front paws and legs stretched down in front, tail wagging, eyes rolling. *Ready?*
I stood near the back patio steps, out of the way. "Go run!"
And he was off. Around the back yard, turn fast at the fence, figure eights to the opposite fence, zoom back to

leap onto the raised patio, leap off, more figure eights. He stopped, but he wasn't finished. *More!* "Go run!" And he was off again.

*That was fun. Did you get good pictures?*

Oh, yes, I did. Feet moving so fast, the camera caught only a blur. Tongue lolling, ears flapping, tail whipping with joy, my Jekyll and Hyde dog.

I downloaded the pictures and printed them.


"That's Dickens?" Lori asked in disbelief. "I can hardly believe it's the same dog." Dickens just grinned at her and put his head in Jason's lap. "Look at these pictures, Jay; your sleepy-eyed, calm, quiet friend looks quite happily berserk."

Jason kept glancing from the pictures to the gentle dog leaning against his legs. "I'll bet he and I could have a rousing game of catch. You know what a baseball is, Dickens?"

*Balls. Round things that people use hands to throw so dogs can catch them and bring them back. We retrievers are very good at catching and bringing back.*

"Jay played baseball for the Navy during the war," Lori told me. "Soon after he finally came home, a Colorado pro baseball team wanted him to try out for them, but he decided to go into the family house-painting business. It made a good life for us, but it was the paint fumes that put him here, where we've been for the past two years."

Jason told me he spent WWII on US Navy ships in the Pacific. He didn't talk about his experiences except to say, "I was lucky. Stayed on the same destroyer for three years. We had a couple close encounters with Kamikazi planes and torpedoes, but only one minor hit."

*What's a cockamamie plane?*

<Not what he said. It's your hearing that is sometimes that way.>

Lori smiled fondly at her husband. "He wrote me many letters, none of which hinted that his time in the Pacific was anything but a pleasant holiday in nice weather. He did propose to me in one of those letters. I immediately sent one back saying yes. We were married a month after he came home. We've been together ever since."

Too few of the wives, other relatives, and friends of the residents ever visit. Lori spends every day from lunch to late afternoon with Jason. Fortunately, the facility has nicely appointed lounges with big windows overlooking patio areas and flower-lined lawns, so folks can escape the tiny half rooms and talk to people, move around.

The residence also has its own salon, where Lori has Linda trim her hair periodically. "At home, Jay used to do it for me," Lori said. "I'd shampoo it in the shower and then he'd come with the clippers and scissors, but now it's easier to have Linda do it all."

Dickens likes to stop and chat with Linda, although he wrinkles his nose at the smell of permanent solution. *She tells me how beautiful I am and how pretty my coat is. She loves me. I love her, too. Friend Beth should have friend Linda do her hair.*

# *Beth*

By the time we got to Beth's room, she'd finished her ice cream and was on to a bag of pretzels. She remembered that Dickens couldn't have one, put the bag aside, took off her glasses, and leaned over for the every Friday face wash.

Of the dozens of Evergreen friends we visit every week, Beth and Gina - and Hank just that one time - are the only ones for whom we break the rules. I don't think doggy kisses are actually forbidden, but I do know many people don't want them. For those who ask, however, Dickens is quite willing to oblige

Dickens did a thorough job on Beth's face. Finally Beth raised her head and went back to stroking the dog's head and shoulders. "I'm glad you're here." She wasn't talking to me.

*I'm glad I'm here, too. But her room sure is cluttered.*

Yes, it was cluttered. In front of the bed a card table held the most recent jigsaw puzzle, which she would finish by the end of the day. If she really liked it, one of the staff would glue it on a piece of thin plywood so it could be hung on the wall. Beth's walls were covered with finished puzzles. Piled high on her windowsill were dozens of stuffed animals.

*When I was little, I'd have played with her toys.*
<Shredded them, you mean.>
*Well that's how puppies play, isn't it? Now that I have manners, I just sniff a hello at them. I wouldn't shred Beth's pets or her slippers or the clothes she leaves on the floor.*

I rarely saw Beth wearing more than a rumpled t-shirt and a Depends as she sat on the bed and suspended the puzzle-solving for a minute. Her hair was also rumpled, bearing a close resemblance to an untidy birds' nest. It wasn't that she forgot; she simply didn't care.

Some days, Beth was content with the face wash alone. This day she wanted to talk. Dickens lay down, sniffing under the bed for errant crumbs before deciding there weren't any.

"They were supposed to drive me down to the house yesterday, but they didn't. The people in there don't belong there, but they said I sold it to them. I wouldn't have done that. I might have said they could stay there until I got out of here. They seemed nice at the time."

Beth talked on. The details changed often, but the basic story had survived for a long time. Beth had lived here at Evergreen for over ten years. Like most of the residents, Social Security paid her expenses, and if there had ever been any income from a house she may or may not have owned, I assumed it was gone.

Beth was still talking, but the drone of the oft-told tale had changed. She sounded excited. "I'm getting out of here. If they won't take me down there, I'll just walk out the door and keep going. I know how to get there and it's not too far."

She'd threatened to leave before, but I didn't doubt that one day she really would simply walk out the door. I wasn't sure what would happen then.

Dickens stood up and shook himself. Beth said, "When I do get back there, Dickens, you and your mom can come and visit. She knows where it is."

*You do?*

<No, I don't, but I'm not going to tell her that.>

*There's a lot of stuff you don't tell our friends. Why?*

<It would make them feel bad if I told them I didn't believe them. Sometimes, they believe things that aren't real, but it does no harm to let them believe, and it could be very harmful to tell them they're wrong. And sometimes, I don't know the facts. So I keep my mouth shut.>

*Huh? You keep talking and you need your mouth open for that.*

<I mean that I don't tell them whether I believe their stories or not. It's important that they feel it's okay to talk about things. It's not important if some of what they say isn't real.>

*Oh. People are weird. Dogs don't think like that.*

A week later, Patsy, the activities director waited for us near the main door. "You will make sure to see Beth, won't you?" Patsy didn't look worried, so I assumed Beth was okay, but I did ask.

"She'll tell you all about it." Now Patsy was stifling a giggle.

# Dickens' Friends

Dickens and I stopped to see the other friends along the way to Beth's room, but we didn't linger with anyone.

*We're going to see Beth? She loves having her whole face washed.*

<Yes. We'll find out what Patsy's talking about.>

Beth sat on the edge of her bed working on yet another jigsaw puzzle. She looked smug. I waited while she put her head down so Dickens could reach every inch of her face with his tongue and she could tell him how wonderful he was. However, the session seemed shorter than usual. When she looked up at me, she said slyly, "Did you hear what I did?"

"No. What did you do?"

"I just walked right out of here and down the street. I was going home."

*Isn't this her home? Did she just run away? That was naughty.*

Beth sat up straight, looking very proud of herself. "Sharon followed me, telling me I had to come back. But I wasn't going back. Next thing I know, a police cruiser pulls alongside and a nice young cop, cute thing he was, says to me, 'Ma'am, it's getting dark and you shouldn't be out here by yourself. Would you get in the car? We'll take you home.' Well, I wasn't born yesterday. I knew he was going to take me back to 'the home,' not my home. But I was getting tired and hungry and a bit cold, so I figured I'd go another day. I asked if they'd put the siren on when they drove up to the door, but they said they couldn't do that."

*I know about dog catchers, police that pick up lost dogs and get them back to their homes, but I didn't know the police were people catchers, too. I mean, I know they catch bad guys and lost kids, but my licky lady?*

<You watch too much TV.>

*Only when you turn it on.*

Beth's jaw jutted out as she ended the story. "Sharon said if I do that again, they'll put a monitor on me. I'd like to see them try. Next time, I'll go out the back door."

During nearly every visit for the next several months, Beth continued to tell us about her intention to sneak out and go home. Then three things changed. First, she started meeting us near the main door, wheeling along in her chair and occasionally talking to one or two other residents.

Then she made friends with the nastiest woman in the place who, the first time we encountered her, said in a very loud voice, "I hate dogs. They aren't supposed to come in here. I'm calling the health department." Patsy evidently told her that we were approved visitors, so when she saw us coming, she gave us a look designed to kill, scooted into her room, and slammed the door.

The third thing was that Beth had Linda style her hair every week and started wearing real clothes – very nice clothes. She looked years younger and quite attractive. Could Beth have a boyfriend? Unlikely. Her friendship with Martha had brought about a stunning transformation.

*She even smells good. But she spends too much time with that nasty lady and isn't always waiting for me to come and wash her face. Maybe she'll get nasty lady to start liking me?*

When pigs fly. Or maybe she and Martha will run away together, I thought to myself.

# Cap

Routine is vital to the smooth operation of health care centers. Something as seemingly simple as ice cream cones on Friday afternoons can make the difference between contentment and agitation. Ice cream is a line item in Evergreen's budget. However, Murphy's law operates even here. One Friday, the ice cream truck broke down, miles away. Popsicles came to the rescue. Not everyone calmly accepted the substitutes. A few were thrown with excellent aim at the frazzled program director, nurses, and aides, although most disgruntled residents merely grumbled and sulked.

Usually there is no knowing what sets off an incident. Cap is a favorite of the staff. Not because he's a sweet, gentle soul. He looks like pictures of a stern Father Winter – long, white beard and ice-blue eyes that can twinkle or shoot angry darts. He's opinionated and gruff. And he loves Dickens.

We met him in the hall one Friday, spinning his wheel chair in agitation.

*Cap is upset. Not at us, but something serious.*

<Maybe if he sees you, he'll calm down.>

*Okay. I'll put my head in his lap. That usually works.*

It did. Cap's clenched fists and mouth relaxed and

the expression in his eyes softened. "Dickens, you're a good boy. But this is a bad, sad day." Cap looked up at me, one hand still stroking Dickens' head as if to calm both himself and the dog. "The court martial is today. I have to testify. So I have to go now, but thanks for coming."

He carefully maneuvered his wheelchair around us, but then took off too fast for safety. Kristin, one of the aides, caught up with him and attempted to calm him down. "Let me go!" he shouted. "I can't be late." Kristin caught sight of us standing several yards away and gestured.

*I can help.*

<Are you sure?>

*No, but we have to try.*

We quickly walked forward, Dickens for once ahead of me rather than in the proper heel position. I was not at all sure we could do anything helpful.

Kristin said, "Cap, Dickens wants to see you."

We all held our breath.

Dickens padded slowly ahead to get alongside Cap's wheelchair and pushed his nose under Cap's elbow. The man's fist tightened and I started to pull my dog away from the blow I was sure was coming.

*Let me help.*

Slowly the tension in Cap's body released, the fist became the familiar caressing hand, and Cap smiled. "Let's go get this old sailor some coffee, Dickens." He looked at Kristin with a challenge in the blue eyes. "Okay if my friend comes in the dining room?"

## Dickens' Friends

The dining room is one of the few areas in the place where dogs are not allowed, but who was going to argue with Cap on a bad day?

# *Maxine*

It was neither popsicles nor courts martial that set Marilyn off. It was her Bible, the book of Revelations to be precise. She sat in her doorway, wheelchair blocking the opening, terror in her eyes, resignation in every muscle in her body. "The world is ending today," she declared in a quavery but certain voice. "What will happen to Dickens?"

*What's she mean? It's a beautiful day, the sun is shining, the rabbits are running, and it's a happy day!*

<You tell her.>

Dickens put a paw on her knee, knowing full well he's not supposed to do that, getting her attention as he furiously wagged his tail and gazed into her face with a full golden grin – tongue out, looking as if he was laughing.

Marilyn's frown eased and she started to smile, unable to resist the invitation to play, or at least cheer up. She glanced at me, down at the Bible on her lap, and back up at me. "Not today?"

"No, Marilyn," I assured her. "It's much too nice a day. No floods, no storm clouds, no pestilence. It's a happy day that the Lord has made for us to enjoy."

"Oh," she said in a note of wonder. "Well, that's all

right then. Thank you for coming. You'll come again?"

"Yes."

"With Dickens?"

"Oh, yes. I couldn't come without him."

*And I couldn't come without you.*

<That's really sweet of you to say.>

*Well, it's true. And anyway, I don't know how to drive.*

# *Betsy*

Until she moved into a private room in the hospice wing, whenever we saw Betsy, she was either on her way to have her hair done, being wheeled off to the bathing room, or scooting down the hall to one of the many activities designed to keep residents engaged. She especially liked the three o'clock happy hour. She was always delighted to see Dickens, spending at least a few minutes petting him and talking to him, but she was a very socially active lady.

*I don't want to see her.*

<Why not? You've always liked Betsy.>

*Because gone friend Rachel got all different when she moved. Before, she was funny and told great stories and was pretty. After, she smelled bad and she wheezed and I just wanted to curl up with her and help her breathe.*

<Maybe Betsy will be more like Hank, really sick but still cheerful and with lots of stories.>

*Will Betsy get all better like Hank did?*

<It's always possible. And she really needs to see us. For now, she can't go wheeling off down the halls to spend time with her friends. They have to come to her.>

*Okay. But if she isn't the same, I'm gonna whine.*

*She's happy! And she really likes this room. She can look out the window and watch the birds and the squirrels. She doesn't have a grumpy, sick roommate like the last one.*

And, I thought to myself, no worry about a roommate dying overnight; there'd been three in the last two months.

Apart from the oxygen tank beside her chair and the plastic tubing leading to her cannula, Betsy hadn't changed. "You scared us," I told her.

"Scared myself. Three bouts of pneumonia and two of them put me in the hospital for a few days. Didn't think I was going to come out the last time. Mary told me you and Dickens came looking for me once or twice.

"I'm glad you're here. For once," she cackled, "we can have a real conversation, can't we, Dickens? I don't have to go anyplace; got my bath and my hair done yesterday."

*Should I lie down while you two talk? If you get boring, I'll have a nap.*

"You stay right here, Dickens. I can pet you and talk to your mom at the same time. I have to admit, much as I love having anyone visit, you're my favorites. You know why? Because you listen!"

Listen we did. I asked a few questions to get her started and then sat down to hear whatever she wanted to tell us about her life.

"Born and raised on a farm in Iowa, me and my brothers and sisters didn't know much about the Great Depression – no leaping off of tall buildings for us! Haystacks and barn lofts, more likely. And Iowa wasn't hit as hard as states north and west of us by the dust bowl years, so our farm did okay. We struggled, of course, but that's farm life. And we had fun. Us kids – there were five of us, two boys and three girls, not that you could tell which was which just looking at us with our overalls and dirty faces – we collected eggs and slopped pigs and let the cows out to pasture and led them back in for milking. And we played hide and seek, and Red Rover come over, and king of the hill, and kick the can. Dad put up an old basketball hoop and we all got pretty good – good enough for the high school boys' and girls' teams. It helped that we were all pretty tall.

"School? Oh, yes. Up through eighth grade we went to the one-room schoolhouse about two miles away. All five of us at one time, Byron in seventh grade, Lucy in fifth, me and Jerome, my twin, in third, and baby Judy in first. And a dozen or more other kids from neighboring farms. We had two teachers, which was enough. They were good.

"After eighth grade, kids had to go into town to the big high school. There were 15 kids in just one grade. We could've walked, except in winter, but our folks got together and bought a bus and Johnny Ulrich's dad drove it.

"You ever live on a farm? No? Well, city folks figure farmers get up with the chickens, work and get dirty all day, eat a big supper, and go to bed before dark. They're wrong. Dinner time at noon was always a big party. The hired hands and all of us would talk – not with our mouths full, of course – about the weather, the crops, which cows were ready to calve, what the Germans were up to, what we'd do if they ever landed in the United States, and how our boys were finally winning back Pacific islands.

"After dinner, we listened to the radio – the news, of course, and The Lone Ranger, the Green Hornet, the Shadow . . ."

I had to say the magic words my brother and I had chanted all those long years ago: "'Who knows what evil lurks in the hearts of men? The Shadow knows!'"

"God, are you that old!" Betsy said. "I wouldn't have guessed. You must have been really healthy as a kid. I wasn't. Rheumatic fever. Spent a year in bed listening to soap operas."

"Oxydol's Own Ma Perkins?" I asked.

"Oh, sure. All of those old serials that went on forever and never got resolved. Most of them are still going, on television now. Some names have changed, that's all."

I showed Betsy the pictures of the previous Saturday's birthday party for Jules, my five-year-old great grandson, and explained how our family sang the birthday song – awful enough so that when Jules first heard it when he was about six months old, his anguished howls could be heard a block away.

"We loved parties, too," Betsy said. "Birthdays, anniversaries, christenings, holidays, and Icelandic Independence Day."

"That's a new one. When is it?"

"August second. It was also my dad's birthday. He wasn't Icelandic – Norwegian, actually, second generation American – but it was a good excuse for a party."

"When's your birthday, Betsy?"

"Christmas Day. Until I got married, I never got an actual birthday present. Never seemed quite fair."

"What's not quite fair?" Mary, one of the many aides looking after Betsy, stuck her head in the doorway.

"Someone always interrupting me just when I'm in the middle of a story," Betsy said with a smile, to let Mary know she wasn't serious.

Betsy was looking tired, so we got ready to leave. "We'll be back," I said.

"I'll be here."

*She will be, you know. She's okay with whatever comes next, but she's not done living.*

I'm praying that Betsy will be here for her Christmas birthday party. Her story is not yet ended.